First published in the United States
of America in 1990 by The Mallard Press

Mallard Press and its accompanying design
and logo are trademarks of BDD Promotional
Book Company, Inc.

Produced by
Twin Books
15 Sherwood Place
Greenwich, CT 06830

ISBN 0 792 45403 0

Printed in Hong Kong

DISNEY'S
MICKEY MOUSE
IN
THE PHANTOM BLOT

Written by
Lee Nordling

TWIN BOOKS

MALLARD PRESS

Raindrops dripped down Mickey Mouse's face as he walked into the police station. The rain had soaked him, but he didn't care. Mickey was furious!

Earlier that evening, someone had sneaked into his house and smashed his brand-new camera. He hadn't even taken a picture yet, and now it was in more pieces than Humpty Dumpty on his living-room floor.

Mickey was determined to find out who had done it—and why!

7

Mickey told Police Chief O'Hara what had happened. When Mickey finished, O'Hara walked over to a closet and opened the door. Out fell dozens of broken cameras.

"It's a crime wave, Mickey," said the chief, "and we're stumped! Why would someone break into houses all over town just to ruin a bunch of cheap cameras?"

"Are all the cameras the same?" asked Mickey.

"Yes," said O'Hara, holding up an unbroken camera. "They're all just like this one that I bought for my grandson. They even came in on the same boat—the *Far, Far East*. What do you think?"

CHIEF O'HARA

the Daily

INVENTION
STILL
MISSING
INVENTOR CLAIMS 3-D
PROCESS REALLY WORKS!

"I think I'm on the case," said Mickey.

Mickey had helped the police figure out some confusing cases in the past, but the motive for these camera crimes was as fuzzy to him as cotton candy. He had taken the chief's unbroken camera and was studying it. Like his own, it was a plastic shell with a plastic lens and red plastic buttons. There was nothing special about it—except that someone would probably want to break it.

Mickey was thinking so hard about his new case that he didn't notice he was being followed.

But when Mickey walked under a street lamp, he saw a shadow in front of him that wasn't his. He spun around.

Nothing was there. Mickey laughed at his own nervousness and turned back. Then he gasped.

In front of him stood a pitch-black figure with piercing eyes. "Give me the camera," it said.

Mickey stepped back, but not quickly enough. The figure grabbed the camera.

"Wh—wh—who are you?" stammered Mickey.

"I'm the Phantom Blot," the figure answered. The Blot took Mickey's picture, then growled when he saw the instant photo that popped out of the camera. He threw the camera to the ground, smashing it into pieces.

13

Mickey looked up from the broken camera and discovered that he was alone. One moment the Phantom Blot was there; the next moment, he wasn't. Mickey shivered, picked up the broken camera and rushed home.

Once there, he took the camera down to the basement and examined it at his workbench. Finally, he came to a conclusion. His camera and Chief O'Hara's were exactly the same. Neither was the one the Phantom Blot was looking for. What *was* the Phantom Blot looking for?

15

Next morning, the newspaper's front page was full of stories about the broken cameras. Mickey read each story twice, but he didn't learn anything new.

Then another story caught his eye. It was about a jewel theft several weeks before in Japan. The thief described sounded an awful lot like the Phantom Blot. The Japanese police had tried to find the thief, but he had disappeared.

Mickey nodded his head. He knew from firsthand experience that the Blot could disappear whenever he wished.

Mickey figured he'd get some answers from the captain of the *Far, Far East.*

Mickey soon found the man he was looking for.

"Aye," said Captain Huf. "We had unloaded a single box of fifty cameras when the ship's fire alarm went off. We rushed around looking for a fire to put out, but we couldn't find one. When we came back to finish unloading the cameras, we discovered that all of them had been taken out of the boxes and smashed."

"All except the first box of fifty?" said Mickey.

"Aye," said the captain.

"And where did you send those?" Mickey asked.

19

Captain Huf's directions led Mickey to a warehouse. There a man gave Mickey the names and addresses of all the stores that had bought the cameras. Mickey hurried off like Pluto after a bone. He figured that the Blot had also learned about the stores.

Cameras had been smashed at all the stores on the first half of the list. Mickey decided to start at the end of the list. Somewhere in the middle, he would meet the Blot. This time he would be ready.

When Mickey stepped into Sam's Camera Shop, he saw a huddled figure searching the shelves.

"Excuse me," said Mickey. "I'm looking for a camera."

The figure at the counter turned around. "So am I!" said the Phantom Blot.

"YOU!" exclaimed Mickey. "You won't get away with this!"

"And you, my friend," said the Blot as he reached over and grabbed Mickey, "will never get away at all."

Mickey struggled, but he was soon tied up tighter than one of Minnie's birthday presents. The Blot found two of the cameras in the store. He took a picture with each of them, snarled at the results and smashed the cameras.

"If you want a better picture," said Mickey, "why don't you try stealing a better camera?"

"I shall tell you a secret," said the Blot. "I have already stolen a better camera. I am just trying to find it." Then the Blot laughed. "I know you will keep my secret," he added. "You will have to."

The Phantom Blot carried Mickey to an empty warehouse in a part of town where there was nothing but empty warehouses. Once inside, Mickey said, "What are you going to do to me?"

"Nothing, my good fellow," said the Blot with a chuckle. "I won't hurt you at all."

"Really?" said Mickey.

"Really," said the Blot, as he propped a ladder against a narrow beam near the ceiling. Then he grabbed Mickey, took him up the ladder, set him on the beam and tied a long rope to his ankles.

"What are you doing?" asked Mickey, as the Blot took the rope from his ankles and tied it to a hook in the ceiling. The Blot wouldn't answer. He just climbed down the ladder, pushed a deep, empty vat underneath Mickey and began to fill it with wet cement.

"You said you wouldn't hurt me!" said Mickey.

"And *I* won't," said the Blot. "Just don't move around, or fall asleep. If you lose your balance, you'll fall headfirst into wet cement. But that wouldn't be *my* fault, would it?"

The Blot left, his laughter ringing in Mickey's ears.

Mickey was stiff and tired from trying to keep his balance. With his wrists tied behind his back, he couldn't work the rope loose. No one answered his cries for help. He had been in tighter spots but at the moment he couldn't remember when.

Mickey looked around for something he might have missed, anything he could use to keep from falling into the wet cement. Finally, he noticed a big nail sticking out of one side of the beam. Mickey smiled, edged his body forward until the nail was close to his collar, then rolled off the beam.

Mickey's collar caught on the nail...and held! Hanging in the air, he tucked up his knees and brought his bound wrists to the front by slipping them under his feet. Then he simply untied the knots with his teeth and freed his hands. After that, it was easy to slip the rope off his ankles, slide partway down the rope and swing clear of the vat.

Mickey dropped to the ground and rushed out of the warehouse. He knew he would have to hurry if he were to pick up the trail of the Phantom Blot.

Back at Chief O'Hara's office, Mickey told the policeman what had happened. Then he showed O'Hara the list of stores that carried the cameras. "How many more of these stores have had cameras smashed, Chief?" Mickey asked.

Chief O'Hara shook his head. "All of them," he said. "Forty-nine cameras have been ruined, and we still don't know why."

Mickey said, "Forty-nine? That means there's one left. I wonder who bought it."

"I did," said Chief O'Hara, holding up the last camera. "I wanted to replace the one I bought for my grandson."

That's when the lights went out.

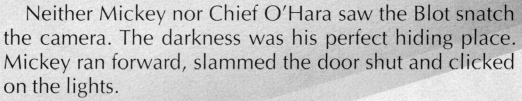

Neither Mickey nor Chief O'Hara saw the Blot snatch the camera. The darkness was his perfect hiding place. Mickey ran forward, slammed the door shut and clicked on the lights.

Near the open window stood the Blot. He aimed the camera directly at a mirror next to the window and snapped a picture. When the picture popped out, the Blot laughed. "At last!" he cried.

The Blot set the picture on the window sill and said, "Figure this out, if you can!" Then he leaped from the window into his waiting car and sped out of sight.

Mickey and O'Hara stared in shock at the window sill. On the sill lay the camera.

When Mickey tried to pick up the camera, it was like trying to grab a handful of smoke. His hand passed right through it. Then a breeze blew the camera off the window sill and flipped it end over end. As it fluttered to the floor, it disappeared. In its place lay the picture the Phantom Blot had taken, upside-down.

Mickey picked up the picture and turned it over. There, in the palm of his hand, was the camera. "This is amazing!" said Mickey.

"What is it?" said Chief O'Hara.

"It's a photograph," said Mickey. "A three-dimensional photograph of a camera that looks just like the real thing. Now I know what the Phantom Blot is up to!"

The next morning Mickey met Chief O'Hara at the Bay City Museum. "Are you sure the Blot will try to steal the Faith Diamond?" asked O'Hara.

Mickey nodded.

"This is the last day of the exhibit," Mickey said. "That's why the Blot was in such a hurry to find the camera."

"I don't get it," said the chief. "What's the diamond got to do with the camera?"

"Everything," said Mickey. "Hurry. We've got to hide before the Blot gets here." They hid behind a pillar as a crowd began to gather around the Faith Diamond.

"How can the Blot try anything with all these people around?" asked the chief.

"He's making his move right now!" said Mickey, leaping forward.

A tall, bearded photographer was moving the diamond to a different position. Mickey tackled him and ripped off his disguise.

"I've got you now, Blot!" said Mickey. "Give up the diamond."

"But the diamond's right there," said the guard, pointing to the display.

"That's a photograph," said Mickey, reaching into the Blot's pocket. "Here's the Faith Diamond!"

Soon the Phantom Blot was safely behind bars, and Mickey told Chief O'Hara how he had figured out the Blot's plot.

"When the Blot left that 3-D snapshot, all the puzzle pieces fell into place. I had read a newspaper story about the camera that took the shot. The Blot needed the camera to take a picture of the Faith Diamond and switch the photo with the jewel, just as he had done in Japan.

"Aboard the *Far, Far East,* the Blot hid the 3-D camera inside a normal camera. When he couldn't find it later, he had to check every camera in the shipment. He destroyed each camera when he was sure he hadn't found the right one."

"That was a great piece of detective work, Mickey," said the chief.